DATE DUE

BRODART, CO.   Cat. No. 23-221-003

Who's in Love with Arthur?

A Marc Brown ARTHUR Chapter Book

Who's in Love with Arthur?

Text by Stephen Krensky

Based on the teleplay by Peter K. Hirsch

Little, Brown and Company

Boston   New York   Toronto   London

Text has been reviewed and assigned a reading level by Laurel S. Ernst,
M.A., Teachers College, Columbia University, New York, New York;
reading specialist, Chappaqua, New York

ISBN 0-316-11539-8 (hc)
ISBN 0-316-11540-1 (pb)
Library of Congress Catalog Card Number 98-66009

10 9 8 7 6 5 4 3 2 1

WOR (hc)
COM-MO (pb)

Published simultaneously in Canada by Little, Brown & Company
(Canada) Limited

Printed in the United States of America

For the Krensky family: Steve, Joan,
Peter, and Andrew

Chapter 1

Outside Lakewood Elementary School, it was raining hard. But inside the gym, it was nice and dry, and the students were dancing to country music. Square dancing was a school tradition on rainy days.

Mrs. MacGrady, who ran the school cafeteria, was their caller. She led them through the different steps.

"Swing your partner round and round," she said. "That's it! Keep swinging."

Arthur and Francine were managing their swing nicely, but not all the couples in their square were as good. As Binky swung Muffy around, her feet kept leaving the ground.

"Not so fast, Binky!" Muffy complained. "I'm not a helicopter."

Mrs. MacGrady clapped her hands. "Side couples! Up to the middle, high five! And now scoot back!"

Binky lumbered forward, yanking Muffy along with him.

"Look out!" she cried as she was hurled off-balance into Francine.

"Hey!" said Francine. "Watch it!"

Muffy slowly picked herself up. "It's not my fault," she said. "Binky threw me!"

Arms swinging madly, Binky hoe-downed backward to his spot. His elbow knocked the Brain to one side. The Brain stepped on Sue Ellen's foot. Sue Ellen slipped and fell onto Francine. In another moment, they were all slipping, falling, and most of all, complaining.

Mrs. MacGrady shut off the boom box.

"I think that's enough for today," she said. "You were all very light on your feet." She glanced at Binky. "And I know the rest of you are trying your best."

Gym was the last class of the day. All the kids returned to Mr. Ratburn's classroom to gather their things before the bell rang.

"Did you say something?" Francine asked Muffy as she passed Muffy's desk.

"No," said Muffy.

After Mr. Ratburn dismissed them, Francine, Muffy, and Arthur headed for the school yard.

"You're doing it again," said Francine.

"Doing what?" asked Muffy.

"Mumbling." Francine folded her arms. "Come on, what's the matter?"

Muffy folded her arms, too. "Well, if you must know, I was just saying what a crummy day this was."

Arthur nodded. "I don't like the rain, either."

"No, not that," said Muffy. "I'm talking about the dancing."

"Oh, that," said Francine, laughing. "You did have your hands full. But I think Binky's getting better."

Muffy snorted. "Maybe so, but I don't know if I'll survive another hoedown like that." She suddenly brightened. "Hey, Arthur! Next time we have square dancing, will you be my partner?"

Arthur shrugged. "Okay," he said.

"Wait a second!" said Francine, frowning. "If you're dancing with Arthur, who's going to be my partner?"

At that moment Binky burst through the door behind them. His shoelaces were untied, and as he came down the steps, he tripped and tumbled to the ground.

Shaking his head, he bounced up a moment later.

"I did that on purpose," he said. "Either that or the step moved."

Muffy smiled at Francine. "And you were wondering about a partner?"

"Oh, no," said Francine. "My health insurance isn't that good. I'm sticking with Arthur."

Arthur looked from one friend to the other. "Don't I get a say in this?" he asked.

"No!" said Francine.

"But—," Muffy started to argue.

"Come on, Arthur," Francine cut in. "I'll give you a lift home."

Francine dragged Arthur away to the street corner, where her father was waiting in his garbage truck. Arthur looked back once, but when he saw the expression on Muffy's face, he didn't look back again.

Chapter 2

• • • • • • • • • • •

Muffy sat down on a bench and sighed. The rain had stopped, and the sun was peeking out from behind the clouds, but that didn't help. Her mood was still dark.

"Boy, do my feet hurt," she said.

"Maybe your shoes are too tight," said Binky, coming up behind her. He had retied his sneakers, but one of the knots was already coming loose again.

"These are very expensive shoes," Muffy explained. "They *envelop my feet in a cocoon of comfort.* It says so right on the box."

"Oh," said Binky, who never thought

about enveloping his feet in anything but socks. "Your feet must be hurting for some other reason, then."

"Yes," Muffy agreed. "Some other reason—like a dancing partner who's always stepping on my toes."

Binky nodded. "Not very considerate. You should tell—hey, that couldn't be it. I mean, *I* was your dancing partner."

"I know."

Binky looked confused. "But I didn't feel a thing."

"I *know*," Muffy repeated.

"Huh," said Binky, scratching his head. "I guess I don't know my own strength."

Muffy sighed. "That's okay. I know you're doing the best you can."

"That's right," said Binky.

"But when Mrs. MacGrady says 'Swing your partner,' she doesn't mean my feet should leave the floor."

"I noticed no one else was doing it my

way. I just figured their partners weren't strong enough."

Muffy stood up and began to pace. "It's not really your fault, Binky. The one I should be mad at is Francine."

Binky nodded. "She stepped on your toes, too, huh," he said knowingly.

"No, no, she's a good dancer. It's just that she won't share Arthur with me. I mean, he's not her personal property. So why should she get to decide who he dances with? The way she acts, you'd think they were married or something."

"Married?" said Binky, horrified. "No way!"

Muffy rolled her eyes. "Well, of course they're not *really* married. But Francine sure acts like she owns him. And she wasn't afraid to tell me to keep my hands off!"

"Francine always speaks her mind," Binky agreed. "I never have to wonder what she's thinking, because she always lets me know. But she's good at sharing. So why won't she change partners with you?"

Muffy looked sideways at Binky. "Hmm, I wonder. Well, I'd better get going. I've got ballet class in an hour." She glanced down. "My feet are going to *love* that."

As Muffy rode off on her bike, Binky stood for a moment, thinking.

Suddenly his eyes grew wide. There *could* be one reason Francine wouldn't want to share Arthur. It would also explain why they went off arm in arm.

"Wow! I guess Arthur and Francine must be in love." Binky shuddered. "I think I'm going to be sick."

Chapter 3

•••••••••••

As Arthur rode his bike to school the next morning, he was still thinking about the day before. Something was going on between Muffy and Francine — that much was certain. However, it was something he didn't quite understand. Of course, there were times when it was safer not to understand these things. The problem was figuring out which times were which.

Binky waiting for him at the bike rack.

"Hi, Binky," said Arthur.

"Good morning, Loverboy. Where's your girlfriend?"

"My what?"

"Your girlfriend."

Arthur folded his arms. "What girl-friend?" he asked.

"I'll give you a little hint. Her initials are F.F."

Arthur blinked. He only knew one person with those initials. "You can't mean Francine?" he said.

"Of course that's who I mean. Don't you even know your own girlfriend's initials?"

Arthur put his hands on his hips. "Francine is not my girlfriend! That's the most ridiculous thing I've ever heard."

"Oh, don't worry. Your little secret is safe with me."

"It's not a secret. THERE'S NOTHING TO HAVE A SECRET ABOUT!"

Binky winked at him. "I get you, Arthur."

"No, you don't," said Arthur, shaking his head as he walked away. Sometimes, it was easier not to argue with Binky.

"ARTHUR AND FRANCINE SITTING IN A TREE," Binky bellowed after him. "*K-S-N-I* . . . Wait a minute. Is that *K-S-I* . . . Oh, well. YOU KNOW WHAT I MEAN!"

Arthur didn't even turn around.

Arthur was still shaking his head when he got to his locker. He looked over at Francine, who was three lockers away. The thought of him and her, the two of them together, was ridiculous. Absurd. Silly. Goofy. In fact, when he stopped to really think about it, the idea was pretty funny.

"Hey, Francine!" he said. "Wait till you hear what Binky just told me. He thinks—"

Francine reached into her locker. "Hold on, Arthur," she said. "I've got a surprise for you. Look!"

She fished out two cowboy hats. "I found them in our basement. My uncle in Texas sent them to us last year."

"Wow!" said Arthur. "They look real."

Francine nodded. "Yep. I'm sure they've seen a lot of time out on the range, rounding up the little dogies."

"Doggies?"

"No, dogies. That's cattle," Francine explained. "Don't ask me why. Anyway, I thought we could wear them the next time there's a square dance."

She plunked one on her own head and gave the other to Arthur.

"Care to dance, pardner?" she asked.

Arthur put the hat on and tugged at the brim. "Be right proud, ma'am."

They laughed and did a little twirl. As Arthur spun around, he saw Binky at the end of the hall. He was whispering to the Brain. At first the Brain looked shocked. Then he started to laugh.

Suddenly Arthur stopped twirling.

"Whoa, pardner!" said Francine. "Give a gal a little warning next time."

"Sorry," said Arthur. "I was, um, getting a little dizzy."

"Okay. By the way, what was it you wanted to tell me? Something about Binky, I think."

"Oh, it's not important. I'll tell you later."

He gave the cowboy hat back to Francine and hurried into the classroom.

Chapter 4

• • • • • • • • • • •

Later that afternoon, Francine and Muffy were changing clothes in the girls locker room. They were getting ready to play baseball.

"See you on the field," said Muffy.

"Hey, Muffy," said Francine. "I've got a new glove to break in today. Do you want to use my old one? It's the best!"

Muffy knew how much Francine liked her old glove, but that didn't mean *she* had to like it.

"I don't think so, Francine. It's used."

"Of course, it's used. That's what makes it so good! This glove has been in the middle of some pretty amazing plays. It snags balls like a magnet."

Muffy inspected it. "Too bad my hand's so small. I don't think your glove will fit properly."

"Oh, well." Francine shrugged. "Can you give it to Arthur, then? I still have to change my socks and sneakers."

"Sure," said Muffy. She weighed the glove in her hand. "Maybe this will help him catch something."

Outside, Arthur was already in right field. Binky was standing near him in center field. He was making loud kissing noises with his lips.

Arthur turned toward him. "Cut it out, Binky. I'm telling you for the last time, nothing is going on between Francine and me."

"Yeah, right. You were holding her hand all during the dance yesterday."

"We didn't have much choice about

that. Besides, you were holding Muffy's hand, too."

Binky stopped smacking. "Hey, wait a minute," he started to say.

"Besides, if I felt the way you think I do, why would I argue with you?"

"So that I wouldn't know the truth," Binky said triumphantly.

"Well, if I didn't want you to know the truth, why would I do things in public where you could see them?"

Binky was starting to get a headache. He had to admit that Arthur sounded pretty convincing. What he needed was more evidence.

"Oh, Arthur!" Muffy came running up to him. "I've brought you Francine's glove."

Arthur looked surprised. "Her special glove? The one she won the championship with?"

"That's right." Muffy handed it to him.

"She really wants you to use it. Here. Try it on."

Arthur took the glove carefully. The inside of the pocket was dark where all the balls had hit it. There was a lot of history in this glove. He couldn't believe Francine would share it with him. Unless . . .

"Ooooooh, Arthur!" cooed Binky. His doubts had all been swept away. Francine would never have let *him* use her glove in a million years. But it seemed that Arthur was different. Special, even. Now Binky had all the proof he needed.

"Cut it out, Binky," Arthur warned.

"There's nothing to cut out, Arthur." He pointed to the pitching mound.

Arthur followed his finger. Francine was standing there. She smiled and waved at him.

"How does it fit?" she called out.

Arthur held up the glove and weakly waved back. "Fine," he said.

Francine laughed. "Only the very best for my pardner!"

Arthur's stomach flip-flopped. Could Binky possibly be right? He knew he wasn't in love with Francine. But what if . . . No, Francine couldn't be in love with him.

Or could she?

Chapter 5

. . . .

Arthur was sitting in a booth at the Sugar Bowl. He was drinking a milk shake and waiting for Francine to arrive. He took the paper from his straw and tied it into a knot. Then he tried to untie it. The knot was being stubborn.

Arthur had made a decision. The best thing to do was to get everything out into the open. There was probably nothing to worry about. It was all in his imagination.

Arthur took a sip of his milk shake. Of course, it was easy enough to think all that. Believing it was another story.

When Francine came in, she hurried over and sat down in his booth.

"Hello, Mr. Secretive."

"Mr. Secretive?"

She nodded. "Arthur, you told me to meet you here and not tell anyone. You said to make sure I wasn't followed and to double back on my tracks. I feel like a spy."

"Okay, okay, so I want us to have a little privacy. That's not such a big deal."

Francine snorted. "If it's not such a big deal, then why —? Oh, never mind. Anyway, I'm here. So, what's this big question that you wanted to ask *in private?*"

Arthur took a deep breath. He was pretty satisfied that no one was eavesdropping. He didn't want to be overheard.

"Um, Francine . . ."

He pushed away his milk shake, trying to collect his thoughts.

"Hey, are you going to finish that?" she asked.

Arthur shook his head.

Francine grabbed a new straw and put it in Arthur's shake.

"Now, as I was saying . . . there's something we should probably discuss. Francine?"

Francine was slurping the milk shake.

"Could you stop slurping for a moment? I'm having a hard time thinking as it is."

Francine pushed the milk shake away. "Sorry. Go on."

Arthur clasped his hands on the table. "Sometimes two people know each other, or at least they think they do. But they really don't know each other as well as they think. I mean, one of them might know them both well, but the other might not. The other one might start getting some funny ideas." He looked at her hopefully. "Understand?"

Francine rolled her eyes. "You must be kidding. I have no idea what you just said."

"All right. Let me put it a different way. Suppose there were these two, um, dolphins. And they did a lot of stuff together. But they didn't think the same way about everything. And one day it happened that—"

A shadow fell on the tabletop. Arthur looked over Francine's shoulder and saw Binky and the Brain outside the window. They were staring at him and Francine. At least they were for a moment. When they saw Arthur looking at them, they gazed at each other, clutched their hearts, and batted their eyes. Then they looked back at Arthur again.

"What about the dolphins, Arthur?" Francine asked impatiently.

Arthur was still looking out the window. Now Binky and the Brain were doubled over, laughing.

Suddenly Arthur stood up. "Oh, nothing! Forget I ever said anything. Bye."

He threw some money on the table for the milk shake and raced out the back door.

Francine looked puzzled. She finished the milk shake with a frown on her face. Boys could be very strange sometimes, and Arthur was no exception.

Chapter 6

• • • • • • • • • • •

That night Arthur called Buster on the phone.

"I need some advice," he said.

"Gee, Arthur, you sound so serious."

"That's because I need serious advice."

"Okay. Let me get serious, too. I'll just put on my serious hat and spin the propeller."

Arthur told him what had happened. When he was finished, Buster was silent for a moment.

"You're kidding, right?" he said finally.

"No, no. I wish I was, but I'm not."

"Because," Buster went on, "it's really hard for me to tell if you're kidding over the phone. I mean, I can't see your face. Your face always gives you away, Arthur. But since I can't—"

"BUSTER!" Arthur shouted. "Trust me. I'm not kidding. I'm very serious."

"In that case," said Buster, "it's just too . . ."

He started to laugh.

"You . . . Francine . . . I mean . . ."

"That's what I thought, too," said Arthur. "At least at first. It seemed like we were just good dancing partners. But that wasn't enough for her. She brought in matching cowboy hats. And then she let me use her old baseball glove."

Buster stopped laughing. "That's true," he remembered. He had been at the game.

"I don't know what's coming next. Do you think I should be worried?"

"It's hard to know with girls," said Buster. "They can be very mysterious. Maybe you'd better keep away from her."

"How can I do that?" asked Arthur. "Francine is one of my best friends."

"Yeah, but what if she tries to kiss you?"

Arthur gulped. "What?"

"That's what girls do when they like you."

"You're making that up."

"No, no, I heard some of the fifth graders talking one day at lunch."

Arthur slumped down in his chair. His eyes were open in shock.

"Arthur!" Buster called out. "Are you okay? Arthur?"

Arthur hung up the phone in a daze. He went up to his room, lay down on his bed, and stared at the ceiling.

Arthur was sitting on an examination table at the doctor's office. He was shivering, and his body was covered with a red rash. His mother

and father were standing nearby. They looked worried.

"Mr. and Mrs. Read," said the doctor, "I'm afraid I have some bad news. Your son has cooties."

"Oh, no!" cried Mrs. Read. "My baby!"

She rushed forward to give Arthur a hug.

"Be careful," said the doctor. "He's highly contagious."

"But how could this happen?" asked Mrs. Read. "We try to make sure Arthur eats from all the food groups. And he brushes his teeth morning and night."

"It's not a question of diet or personal grooming," the doctor explained. "Arthur got the cooties from a kiss."

Mrs. Read gasped. "Arthur, is this true?"

"I don't know," said Arthur.

"Has anyone been kissing you lately?"

"Well, Grandma Thora . . ."

The doctor shook his head. "Family doesn't count."

Arthur stopped to think. "Well, then, only Francine."

"And who is this Francine?" the doctor asked.

"A friend," said Arthur. "Just a friend. Honest."

"Is there no cure?" asked Mr. Read.

The doctor shook his head again. "We live in an age of technological wonders." He sighed. "But some things are still beyond the reach of medical science."

So this is what it's like to be doomed, thought Arthur.

It was not a good feeling.

Chapter 7

• • • • • • • • • • •

The next morning Arthur got up slowly.

"C'mon, Arthur," said his father, passing by the bedroom door. "Let's get moving." He took a step back and peered at his son. "Are you feeling okay?"

Unfortunately, Arthur knew that dreaming about a cootie attack was not the same as being sick. "I'm fine," he said. "But I wish I didn't have to go to school today."

Mr. Read nodded. "I used to have days like that. Especially in good weather." He glanced out the window. "But that's not a problem today. It looks like rain."

Arthur groaned. Rain. That meant more dancing.

When he finally made it down to the kitchen, everyone else was already having breakfast. Arthur sat down to eat, but he didn't feel very hungry.

"Mom!" said his sister D.W. "Arthur's playing with his food."

"I am not," said Arthur.

D.W. laughed. "Oh, really!" she said, pointing.

Arthur looked down at his plate. Without even thinking about it, he had re-arranged his scrambled eggs into the shape of a heart.

"It's just your imagination," he said, hastily taking a few bites.

"You do seem a little distracted," said his mother, giving baby Kate her cereal.

"I have a lot on my mind," Arthur admitted.

"Like what?" asked D.W.

"Like what to do about pesky sisters who ask too many questions."

D.W. didn't care. "My teacher says it's good to be curious about things."

Arthur sighed. "Yeah, but sometimes you can find out things it would be better not to know."

When Arthur got to school, he saw Muffy, Buster, Sue Ellen, and the Brain. He didn't see Francine.

Maybe she's home sick, he said to himself. Not that he wanted her to really feel bad or anything. He just wasn't sure he wanted to face her in gym class.

He was just closing the door to his locker when someone tapped him on the shoulder.

"Aaah!" Arthur shouted.

"Bit jumpy this morning, aren't you?" said Francine.

"Oh, it's you." Arthur backed up a step. "I thought maybe you were sick today."

"No, I just got a ride. I slept late. I had the weirdest dreams last night."

"Me, too," said Arthur. Then he brushed off his shoulder where Francine had touched him. He didn't know that much about cooties, but it was better not to take any chances.

Francine gave him a look. "Are you all right?"

"Fine. Great. Super. Wonderful."

He started down the hall.

Francine followed him. "Is something wrong, Arthur? You've been acting a little strange."

He put his hand on the bathroom door.

"Wrong?" said Arthur. "Of course not! Why would you think something silly like that?"

"Well, let me see ... You're jumpy. You're nervous. Oh, and there's the fact that you're about to go into the girls' bathroom."

Arthur jerked his hand back from the door.

"Ah . . . I was just kidding. It was a joke."

"If you say so," said Francine. But as far as she was concerned, the joke wasn't very funny.

Chapter 8

Even though Francine thought Arthur was acting strange, she still saved him a seat at lunch.

"Over here, Arthur!" she called out, waving to him across the crowded cafeteria.

Arthur pretended not to see her. He tried to sit at a table of fourth graders. They reluctantly made room for him.

"Thanks," said Arthur. "So, you guys come here often?"

The fourth graders ignored him.

"Did you hear something?" one of them asked.

"I think it was a bug," said another.

"I wish that bug would buzz off," said a third. "I don't like it being here."

"Hey!"

Arthur looked up. Francine was standing beside him.

"Why are you sitting over here?" she asked. "I was saving you a seat. Didn't you see me waving?"

"Oh, well, I guess I wasn't paying attention. Anyway, I thought I would meet some new friends today."

The fourth graders snickered.

Francine put her hands on her hips. "Fine. See if I care. I'm going back to my lunch. I don't want it to get cold."

She turned sharply and left.

Arthur smiled at the rest of the table. "She's a friend. Not a girlfriend or anything like that. Just a friend who happens to be a girl. That makes sense, doesn't it?"

The fourth graders stared at him.

When Francine returned to her table, Prunella could see something was wrong.

"What's the matter?" she asked.

Francine shook her head. "Arthur is what's the matter. He's acting really strange around me."

Prunella was interested. "Like how?"

"Whenever I try to talk with him, he makes excuses to get away. Except yesterday, when he insisted I meet him in private at the Sugar Bowl."

"Hmmm . . ." Prunella had an idea. "Tell me something. Do his cheeks get red at these times?"

Francine stopped to think. "Yeah, I guess they do."

"And does he hesitate a lot when he talks?"

Francine nodded.

"Well, then," said Prunella, "I think I know what's going on."

"You do?"

"I hate to say this, Francine, but I think Arthur is in love with you."

Francine almost fell over. "WHAT! Arthur? With me? That's ridiculous."

Prunella shrugged. "I'm sorry, but he's showing all the signs."

Francine made a face. "That's the grossest thing I've ever heard."

"It's quite common, really. Usually it shows up in older boys. Arthur may just be a little ahead of himself."

"Why me, though? Am I so irresistible?"

Prunella sighed. "It's a burden, I know. And with that burden comes responsibility."

"What do you mean?"

"Well, you have to tell Arthur the truth — that you don't love him. But you also have to be careful. You don't want to break his heart."

"You're right," Francine agreed.

"That means finding a quiet, private

moment to share your feelings. It's a delicate situation."

Francine looked across the cafeteria at Arthur. He was not looking back. He was just staring down at his plate.

The poor guy, she thought. I'll have to be very gentle with him.

Chapter 9

• • • • • • • • • • •

Arthur approached the gym in slow motion. His hands were clammy, and the sweat was gathering on his forehead. He didn't need a crystal ball to predict that the next hour was going to be a disaster. He just knew.

As expected, Mrs. MacGrady was preparing to lead everyone again in dancing. The kids gathered at one end of the gym.

Arthur and Francine nervously faced each other.

"Well, here were are," said Arthur.

"Yes," Francine agreed. "Here we are, all right."

"I don't see the cowboy hats."

"No," said Francine. "I guess I left them behind. I could run back and get them—if you want."

"No, no," said Arthur. "Anyway, I've been thinking."

"Me, too," Francine added quickly.

"Have you been thinking about the same thing that I have?"

"I don't know. What were you thinking about?"

Arthur hesitated. "Well, what were *you* thinking about?"

"You first."

"Okay," said Arthur. "Maybe we shouldn't dance—"

"With each other," Francine finished for him.

Arthur looked relieved. "Right!" he said.

"Okay," said Francine.

They looked around for other partners. Arthur paired off with Muffy, while Francine stood next to Binky.

"All right, cowboys and cowgirls," said Mrs. MacGrady. "Let's see how much you remember from our last hoedown."

She turned on the boom box.

"Bow to your corner, and bow to your partner," she said.

Everyone bowed smoothly, except Binky, who bent down a little too far and knocked his head against Francine's.

"Ow! Binky!"

"Sorry."

"Look, Binky," said Francine, as they waited for Mrs. McGrady's next call. "You have to be careful. I only have these two feet, you know. I can't go to the mall and buy replacements."

Binky grinned at her. "I suppose you'd rather be dancing with Arthur."

"I would not! Now, pay attention. Here comes the next move."

Mrs. McGrady clapped her hands. "Now, everybody promenade!"

Binky and Francine walked arm-in-arm around the circle. As they passed Arthur and Muffy, Arthur turned his head to see how they were doing.

Binky smiled. "Jealous?" he asked.

"Arthur!" said Muffy. "We're falling behind. Pay attention!"

She jerked him forward.

Arthur looked straight ahead. He tried to concentrate on dancing with Muffy, but he found himself thinking about Francine. Muffy wasn't a bad dancer, but she didn't have Francine's enthusiasm for square dancing.

"Muffy," Arthur whispered. "Don't you feel like stomping your feet and yelling, 'Yee-ha'?"

"Why would I do that?" Muffy

whispered back. "Every dance has steps to follow. I'm being careful. I have to follow the right ones at the right time."

"Now thread the needle!" said Mrs. MacGrady.

The kids started to form two rows, hands held high to make a tunnel. As the pairs jostled for position, Arthur suddenly found himself face-to-face and hand-in-hand with Francine.

"What are you doing here?" said Arthur. "Quit trying to dance with me."

"*Me* trying to dance with *you? You're* the one trying to dance with *me!*"

"Francine, do I have to spell it out for you?"

"Don't make me say it, Arthur!"

They both took a deep breath.

"I'M NOT IN LOVE WITH YOU!" they said together.

Chapter 10

• • • • • • • • • • • •

For a moment, both Arthur and Francine were stunned. They faced each other open-mouthed.

Francine was the first to find her voice.

"You mean, you don't have a crush on me?" she said.

Arthur's mouth snapped shut. "No way! I don't get crushes. But what about you?"

Francine frowned. "I don't get crushes, either."

"But don't you want to kiss me?"

"Are you kidding? I'd rather have head lice."

"Ewwww, gross," said Prunella, who was standing nearby.

Suddenly Arthur and Francine realized that the dance had ended and everyone was staring at them. This could have been embarrassing. Actually, it was embarrassing. But suddenly both Arthur and Francine realized the whole thing was so ridiculous that they burst out laughing.

"But I thought —," Francine started to say.

"Well, I was positive —," Arthur stammered back.

"Okay," said Mrs. MacGrady. "Show's over. Everyone, grab a partner!"

The music started up again. Arthur turned to Francine. He made a little bow.

"May I have this dance?" he asked.

Francine curtsied back. "Yes, you may."

"What about us?" asked Muffy. Binky was standing beside her.

"Don't worry," said Francine, "you still have—"

"Each other," Arthur finished for her.

"All right, Binky," said Muffy, holding out her hands with a sigh. "Let's try it again."

As Arthur and Francine started skipping around the circle, Francine grinned.

"Whew, I'm glad that's over," she said.

"Me, too," said Arthur. "Let's never let a silly thing like love come between us again."

"You said a mouthful, pardner! If I don't hear the *L*-word again for at least a year, it will be too soon. Now, let's show the rest of these folks how to step out and raise some dust."

And the two friends danced like crazy till the bell rang.